I Wish I'd Been Born a Unicorn

by Rachel Lyon

Illustrated by Andrea Ringli

Mucky was a **playful** horse,
Who lived up to his name.
He didn't **bathe**, or brush his teeth,
And never **combed** his mane.

No other horse would share his field
Because he'd grown so **smelly**,
And **flies** and **fleas** would bite his knees
And picnic on his **belly**.

"I wish I had some friends," he sighed,
while chewing on some hay.
"But no one seems to like me much -
I'm never asked to play."

"If I'd been born a unicorn,
I bet they'd like me more.
But I'm just silly Mucky,
Who likes rolling on the floor."

"Your true friends," said a clever owl
As Mucky ate his meal,
"Aren't bothered how you look or smell,
But only how you feel."

"However, if it's really what you want,
I'll make your wish come true.
I'll help you be a unicorn."
And up and off he flew.

Now, unicorns are white, of course,
And Mucky's brown and plain.
So first, Owl asked the cows for milk
To paint his coat and mane.

"But milk is runny," mooed the cows.
"It simply will not stick!
Perhaps if Frog will swim around,
He'll churn it nice and thick."

Owl headed next towards the beach,
To find a pointy shell,
Which once tied tight on Mucky's head
Would work so very well.

Owl took the **cream** to Mucky's field
And worked the whole night through.
He turned him white from head to hoof,
To make his **dream** come true.

One final touch, between his ears,
He tied the **seashell horn**.
"Come look," Owl cried to all around.
"And see the **unicorn!**"

Up hurried frog, the cows came too,
They waited in the field.
The sun came up and in its light,
New Mucky was revealed.

"A unicorn? Where?" Mucky asked.
"You surely don't mean me?"
"Oh yes," Frog and the cows replied.
"Look in the pond, you'll see."

"I am! I am a unicorn!"
He sang and skipped with glee.
"I'll soon have friends, and best of all,
They'll want to play with me."

But suddenly a cloud appeared.
It slid across the sun.
"It mustn't rain!" thought Little Owl.
"Poor Mucky's coat will run."

The sky grew dark, the wind blew wild,
The raindrops tumbled down.
And right before their very eyes
The unicorn turned brown.

"Oh deary me," the milk cows cried.
"Poor Mucky seemed so glad,
But now the milk's been washed away,
He looks so very sad."

"Dear Mucky, please don't cry", they begged.
"We'll make more cream today,
And once you're painted white again,
We're sure you'll get to play."

But as they looked on, feeling sad,
They saw a smile appear.
It grew on Mucky's dirty face
From filthy ear to ear.

"Who needs to be a unicorn?
Who needs a wish come true?
I'll never feel alone again
With friends as good as you!"

"It's like Owl promised yesterday –
You know your friends are real
When all they truly care about
Is how you really feel."

"I'm glad I'm not a unicorn,"
He added with a neigh.
"I now have all the friends I need,
So let's all go and play!"

The End

I Wish I'd Been Born a Unicorn
is an original concept by © Rachel Lyon

Author: Rachel Lyon

Illustrator: Andrea Ringli

Published by MAVERICK ARTS PUBLISHING LTD
Studio 3A, City Business Centre, 6 Brighton Road,
Horsham, West Sussex, RH13 5BB
© Maverick Arts Publishing Limited September 2014 +44 (0)1403 256941

A CIP catalogue record for this book is available at the British Library.

ISBN 978-1-84886-117-6

Maverick
arts publishing
www.maverickbooks.co.uk